Gone Fishing

Adaptation of the animated series: Anne Paradis
Illustrations: Eric Sévigny, based on the animated series

chouette

"It's time to get up, Caillou," said Daddy. "We don't want to keep the fish waiting."
Caillou had to get up very early to go fishing.
"I'm going to catch lots of fish," Caillou exclaimed.
"Sometimes even good fishermen catch only one fish," Daddy answered.
"Then I'll catch a really big one!"

Caillou heard Grandpa come in. He ran to give him a hug.
"Your hat is funny," Caillou said.
"I always catch fish when I wear this hat," Grandpa explained. "It's my lucky hat."
"I hope you have better luck than last time," Mommy laughed. "You didn't catch a single fish."

When they got to the lake, the fishermen took out their gear.
"Here's your fishing rod and your lucky hat," Grandpa said.
Caillou was thrilled. He felt like a real fisherman.
"I'm ready," said Caillou. "Let's go!"
"First we'll buy some bait for the fish," Daddy said.

Caillou noticed that the feathers in the store were like the ones on Grandpa's hat.
"These are lures and these are flies to attract the fish," Grandpa said.
Daddy came back with bait.
"Worms?" Caillou was surprised.
"Fish love earthworms," Daddy explained. "It's like peanut butter and jam to them."

The fishermen waited patiently for quite a while.
"When are the fish going to come and eat?"
Caillou asked.
"Sh," said Daddy, quietly. "We don't want to scare them away. Fish are used to the sounds of nature. Can you hear them?"
Caillou heard water lapping, a bird twittering and the fluttering wings of a dragonfly.

Caillou also heard the whirr of a fishing reel.
"Look over there! That man caught a fish."
The man gently took his catch off the hook and put it back in the water.
"Why didn't he keep the fish?" Caillou asked.
"That fish was too small," Grandpa explained.
"Now it can grow and become a big fish."

Caillou started to get tired of waiting and having to stay still. Daddy explained, “When you go fishing, you have to be very patient, like Grandpa. He has a lot of experience.” Caillou and Daddy looked at Grandpa. He had fallen asleep! Caillou and Daddy burst out laughing.
“Why don’t we take a break, too?” Daddy suggested.

Daddy and Caillou went to see the fishing boats.
"What are the fishermen going to do with all those fish?" Caillou asked Daddy.
"I guess they'll sell them to the fish store, and people can buy them for dinner."
Caillou wanted to take home a fish for dinner, too. "Let's try to catch one."

Caillou really wanted to catch a fish. He stayed very still and he waited.
Suddenly he felt a tug on his fishing line.
"Daddy, I've got one!"
"Quick, reel it in!" Daddy said.
Caillou reeled in his line. There was a little fish wriggling on the hook, but it fell back into the water.

Caillou was disappointed to lose his fish.
"You'll have better luck next time," Grandpa said, "and by then the little fish will be big."
Caillou was happy that he had gone fishing, even if he hadn't caught anything.
Daddy said, "All this fresh air has made me hungry."
"But we don't have any fish to eat," Caillou answered.

Grandpa had an idea. "Trust me! I have a lot of experience. I know where there are a lot of fish."
When they got home, Caillou gave a package to Mommy.
"Wow, what a beautiful fish!"
Caillou couldn't help laughing.
"We caught it at the fish store!"

Text: adaptation by Anne Paradis of the animated series CAILLOU, produced by DHX Media Inc.

Original story written by Sarah Musgrave and Jason Bogdaneris
Original Episode #190: Gone Fishing
Illustrations: Eric Sévigny, based on the animated series CAILLOU

We acknowledge the financial support of the Government of Canada through the Canada Book Fund for our publishing activities.

Canadian Heritage Patrimoine canadien

We acknowledge the support of the Ministry of Culture and Communications of Quebec and SODEC for the publication and promotion of this book.

SODEC Québec

Bibliothèque et Archives nationales du Québec and Library and Archives Canada cataloguing in publication

Paradis, Anne, 1972-
[Caillou va à la pêche. English]
Caillou: gone fishing!
(Clubhouse)
Translation of: Caillou va à la pêche.
For children aged 3 and up.

ISBN 978-2-89718-183-3

1. Patience - Juvenile literature. I. Sévigny, Éric. II. Title. III. Title: Caillou va à la pêche. English. IV. Series: Clubhouse.

BJ1533.P3P37213 2015 j179'.9 C2014-941243-6

Printed in Canada

10 9 8 7 6 5 4 3 2 1 CHO1925 OCT2014